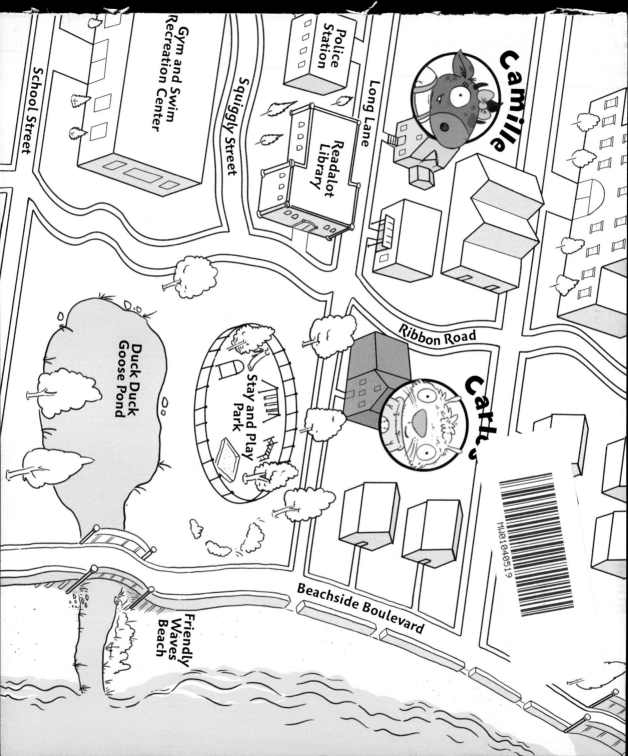

Stuart J. Murphy

Freda Plans a Picnic

Cognitive Skills: Sequencing

Stuart J. Murphy's
I See I Learn

Charlesbridge

Freda *loved picnics!*
One day her mom said that she could have one—
right in her own backyard.

Freda invited Percy, Ajay, and Emma.

"Can I bring Pickle?" asked Emma.

"Sure," said Freda. "Pets can come to picnics."

It was the morning of the picnic.

"First let's **pack** the basket," said Freda's mom.

She put in four big sandwiches, some apples,

and a box of chocolate chip cookies.

"I'll put in four juice boxes," said Freda.
"And here's a special treat for Pickle," said her mom.

pack

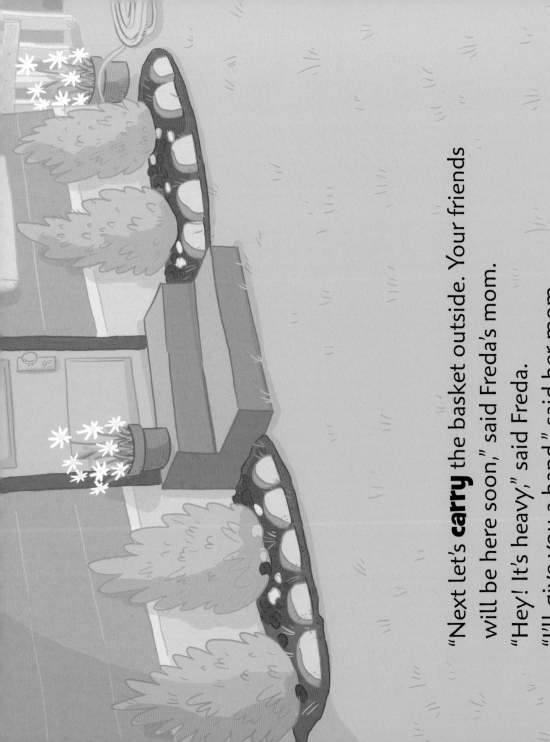

"Next let's **carry** the basket outside. Your friends will be here soon," said Freda's mom.

"Hey! It's heavy," said Freda.

"I'll give you a hand," said her mom.

carry

pack

When they got outside, Freda started to take food out of the basket.

"Not yet!" said her mom as she spread a blanket.

"We're here!" shouted Percy.
Pickle jumped right into the middle of the blanket.

"Now we're ready," said Freda.
She started to **unpack** the basket.

Freda lined up the juice boxes. "Look," said Emma. "There's even a treat for you, Pickle."

unpack

carry

pack

"It's time to **eat** lunch," said Freda.

"Yum," said Ajay as he took a big bite of his sandwich.

"No, no, Pickle!" said Emma. "That's Ajay's sandwich. Your treat is over here."

eat

unpack

carry

pack

"Now it's time for dessert," said Freda.

They crunched their apples and
gobbled up the chocolate chip cookies.
They slurped from their juice boxes
until their straws made funny noises.

"Percy!" called Emma.
"Stop chasing Pickle.
He's getting all dirty."

Just then, Freda's mom came back outside.
"It's time to clean up," she said.

"Aw," said Freda. "We're having so much fun."

"If you all work together," said her mom,

"there's one last thing you can do."

Everyone helped **clean up**.
Even Pickle.
"We're done," said Freda.
"Now, what's the one last thing?"

clean up

eat

unpack

carry

pack

"Pickle needs a cleanup, too!" said Freda's mom.

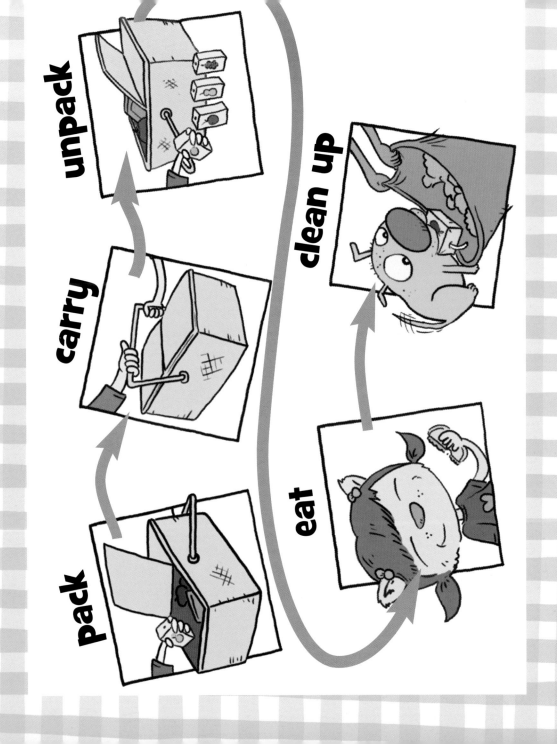

pack

carry

unpack

clean up

eat

A Closer Look

1. How would **you** plan a picnic?

2. Look at the pictures.
   What did Freda do first?
   Next? After that?

3. What did Freda and her friends do together?

4. Which part of the picnic did you like best?
   Why?

5. Pretend you are having a picnic.
   What would you do first?
   Next? After that?

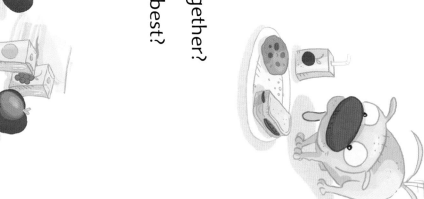

A Note About Visual Learning and Young Children

Visual Learning describes how we gather and process information from illustrations, diagrams, graphs, symbols, photographs, icons, and other visual models. Long before children can read—or even speak many words—they are able to assimilate visual information with ease. By the time they reach pre-kindergarten age (3–5), they are accomplished visual learners.

I SEE I LEARN™ books build on this natural talent, using inset pictures, diagrams, and highlighted words to help reinforce lessons conveyed through simple stories. The series covers social, emotional, health and safety, and cognitive skills.

Freda Plans a Picnic focuses on sequencing, a cognitive skill. The ability to recall events in proper order—what happens first, what comes next, and what occurs last—is important for story comprehension, mathematics, following directions, planning, and other life skills.

Now it's time to help your child plan a picnic!